GO WEST, SWAMP MONSTERS!

by Mary Blount Christian
pictures by Marc Brown

PUFFIN BOOKS

PUFFIN BOOKS
Published by the Penguin Group
Penguin Books USA Inc., 375 Hudson Street, New York, New York 10014, U.S.A.
Penguin Books Ltd, 27 Wrights Lane, London W8 5TZ, England
Penguin Books Australia Ltd, Ringwood, Victoria, Australia
Penguin Books Canada Ltd, 10 Alcorn Avenue, Toronto, Ontario, Canada M4V 3B2
Penguin Books (N.Z.) Ltd, 182–190 Wairau Road, Auckland 10, New Zealand

Penguin Books Ltd, Registered Offices: Harmondsworth, Middlesex, England

First published in the United States of America by Dial Books for Young Readers,
a division of Penguin Books USA Inc., 1985
Published in Canada by Fitzhenry & Whiteside Limited, Toronto, 1985
Published in a Puffin Easy-to-Read edition, 1996

1 3 5 7 9 10 8 6 4 2

Text copyright © Mary Blount Christian, 1985
Illustrations copyright Marc Brown, 1985
All rights reserved

The Library of Congress has cataloged the Dial edition as follows:

Christian, Mary Blount. Go west, swamp monsters!
Summary: Four young swamp monsters put on cowboy clothes
and go in search of the wild, wild West.
1. Children's stories, American. [1. Monsters—Fiction.]
I. Brown, Marc Tolon, ill. II. Title
PZ7.C4528Gb   1985   [E]   84-12686

Puffin Easy-to-Read ISBN 0-14-03.6230-4

Printed in the United States of America

Reading Level 2.3

Reprinted by arrangement with Viking Penguin, a division of Penguin Books USA Inc.

For Jennifer, Christopher,
and Jason

M.B.C.

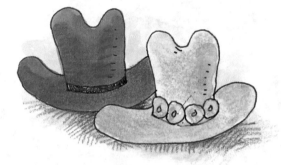

For Haley,
one sweet little cowpoke

M.B.

"Fenny! Crag!
Put away your lizards,"
Mrs. Swamp Monster called.
"We're going
to your cousins' for supper.
Auntie Bog and Uncle Sump
are having a cookout."

"Yummy!" Crag said.

"Swamp burgers and hot frogs!"

"Yeah!" Fenny said. "And toadstools toasted over the fire!"

Crag and Fenny wore their
shiny new spurs.
They pulled their western hats
low over their eyes.

"I'm a tough cowboy,"
Crag told his cousins
when they got there.
"I'm an old cowpoke!"
Fenny clopped like a horse.
Marsh and Swale got out
their western hats too.

"We're big bad cowpokes,"
Marsh said.

Nearby, supper sizzled on the grill.

The swamp monsters played cowboys.

Clinka, clink, clink!

Crag and Fenny's spurs jingled

when they walked.

"I want to wear the spurs now,"
Marsh begged.

"No, they're mine!" Crag screamed.

He yanked a ribbon off her pigtail.

Uncle Sump flipped the meat.

He stabbed the air with his fork.

"Crag and Fenny, share your spurs
with Marsh and Swale!"

Grumbling, Crag gave Marsh
one spur to wear.

Fenny saw Auntie Bog watching.

He took off one spur.

When she was not looking,
he threw it at Swale.

11

"Let's play that Spot is our horse!"
Swale said.

He threw a rope over Spot.

"GRONK!" the gator groaned.

Fenny pushed Swale down.

"Leave my gator alone!"
Fenny yelled.

Marsh threw a mudball at Fenny.

Uncle Sump waved his meat fork.

"You're acting as bad as CHILDREN!"

he yelled.

"No supper for any of you

until you behave like MONSTERS!"

The swamp monsters hid behind
the tall bushes.

"How can Uncle Sump be so mean?"
Fenny cried.

"Let's run away
and never come back.
Then they'll be sorry!"

"Wait," Crag said.

"I have a better idea.
Let's run away
to the wild, wild West."

"Right, pardner!" Swale agreed.

They climbed on Spot's back.

"GRONK!"

"Giddy-up!" Crag yelled.

They rode off into the swamp.

The four monsters rode for a while.

Then they heard a strange noise.

They jumped off Spot

and peeked through the bushes.

Two camping trucks were parked

side by side.

One said:

TROOP TWELVE
OLD WEST CAMP OUT

The other said:

TROOP SIX
OLD WEST CAMP OUT

"It's humans," Fenny whispered.

"Two big ones

and a bunch of little ones.

And they're dressed like us."

"Oh, boy!" Swale said.

"We must be at the wild, wild West."

Marsh and Swale crept closer.

"Mr. Dingle,"

one of the little ones yelled,

"Herman kicked me in the tummy."

"I didn't try to,"

Herman said,

"but you turned around!"

Mr. Dingle blew a whistle,

Tweet, tweeeeeeeet!

"Control your buckeroos,

Ms. Piper," he said.

"Why did you put a frog

down my shorts?" one asked.

The other one shrugged.

"Because I lost my mouse," he said.

"Control *your* buckeroos,"

Ms. Piper said.

Marsh giggled.

Don Dingle stomped over

to the monsters.

"All right, I hear you.

Come on out, little cowpokes.

You must stay with the rest of us.

Don't mosey off in the swamp."

"Yippee!" Swale squealed.

"He thinks we're cowboys.

Let's go!"

The swamp monsters

joined the scouts.

The one called Herman
grinned at them.

"Nice fuzzy chaps," he said.

"Line up, and shake a leg!"
Mr. Dingle said.

"I think he wants
to hear our spurs jingle,"
Fenny said.

Crag and Fenny
and Marsh and Swale
shook their legs.
Clinka, clink, clink!

Ms. Piper sighed.

"I'll handle this," she said.

"Come on, kids.

Let's hop to it!"

"Well, why didn't he say so?"

Crag asked.

The swamp monsters

hopped over to Mr. Dingle.

Herman laughed.

He hopped next to the monsters.

"Just hurry up!" Mr. Dingle yelled.

The troopers formed a line.

The monsters lined up too.

"All right, cowpokes,"

Ms. Piper said.

"Pitch your tents!"

The monsters watched

the children set up their tents.

"That is not what she said to do,"

Crag said.

"We've already been thrown out

of one place today," Fenny said.

"We better do exactly what

we are told."

The four of them picked up a tent.

They pitched it into the swamp.

"Hey! Great idea!" Herman said.

He threw his tent into the swamp too.

Mr. Dingle leaped in after the tents.

"Ms. Piper means, put the tents up!"

he shouted.

"She should say so in the first place,"

Marsh said.

Crag pointed to a tree.

"Is that *up* enough?" he asked.

The swamp monsters climbed the tree.

They dragged the tent behind them.

They hung it on a branch.

Herman put his tent up too.

"We're here to have fun,"

Ms. Piper ordered.

"Now, let's build a campfire."

She piled sticks up and lit them.

The flames leaped high.

Herman twirled his rope and threw it into the fire.

"Don't do that!" Ms. Piper screamed.

She jumped up and down.

"That really burns me up!" she said.

"Quick! We have to help her!"

yelled Marsh.

The swamp monsters

ran to the swamp

and filled their hats.

KER-SPLASH!

They threw the water on Ms. Piper.

Ms. Piper fell to the ground.

"How could you—you—

you little MONSTERS?"

"She called us *monsters*!"

Marsh said proudly.

"Yeah," Crag said.

"Uncle Sump should see us now!"

"Ms. Piper must dry out by the fire,"

Mr. Dingle said.

"The rest of us will roast hotdogs."

While the food cooked,

the children sang.

37

Roasting the hotdogs was fun.

But the swamp monsters

didn't think eating them

was fun at all.

The mustard oozed onto their fur.

And the catsup

dribbled between their toes.

"I want to watch cartoons on TV,"
one boy said.

"Yeah, why can't we camp
at a hotel?" Herman asked.

"We could have room service."

"TV? Hotels?" Crag said.

"Maybe the West isn't so wild
after all."

"I'm tired of being a children,"
Marsh said.

"Especially a cowboy children,"
Swale said.

"I miss Mom and Pop," Fenny said.

"I even miss Uncle Sump,"
added Crag.

Just then Ms. Piper yelled to them.

"It's time for our Old West Roundup."
She stamped her foot.

"Now step on it!"

"If that's what she wants,"
Fenny said.

They all stepped on her foot.

41

"I'm glad you monsters

are in *his* troop," she cried.

Tweeeeet! The whistles sounded.

"Let's go!" shouted Mr. Dingle.

"Get along, little doggie,"

he sang as he marched.

"We don't have a long, little doggie,"

Crag said.

"But we have a long little gator,"
Fenny said. He whistled.

Spot galloped up.

Crag, Fenny, and their cousins
jumped on.

"Hey, wait for me!" Herman called.

He pulled his hat low over his eyes.

He leaped on Spot's back too.

The troops hiked

through the swamp.

When the troops turned right,

Spot turned left.

Soon the swamp monsters

were back home.

Uncle Sump was just dishing up

the hot frogs and swamp burgers.

They smelled so good!

"We went to the wild, wild West,"

Crag told Uncle Sump.

"The people said

we acted just like monsters.

Now can we eat with you?"

"What a story!" Uncle Sump chuckled.

"Out West! People, indeed!"

"Can Herman stay too?" Marsh asked.

"He's okay, for a children."

"A children!" Auntie Bog scolded.

"What a mean thing
to call your friend."

She got a plate for Herman.

Herman took one bite of his hot frog.

"I think I'm not hungry,"

he said, holding his tummy.

In a flash he was gone.

Marsh frowned.

"That's not nice, to eat and run."

"Oh, well," said Crag,

munching on a fried fly.

"I guess cowpokes just don't know

what's good!"

And they all agreed.